Igglepiggle lost!

Andrew Davenport

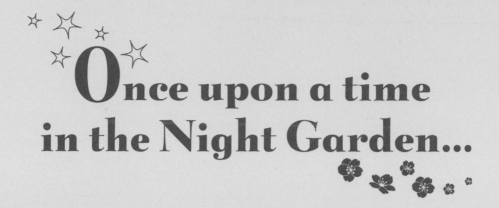

Once upon a time in the Night Garden...

Igglepiggle came to play.

Yes, my name is Igglepiggle,
Iggle-piggle-wiggle-niggle-diggle!
Yes, my name is Igglepiggle,
Iggle-piggle-wiggle-niggle-noo!

One day, Igglepiggle went looking for his friends in the garden.

Upsy Daaaaaiisy!

Upsy Daisy was singing.

Clack-clack-clatter!

Makka Pakka was tidying his stones.

The Tombliboos were playing Tombliboo music.

Plink-plonk-bang!

What a lot of noisy noises, Igglepiggle!

Igglepiggle walked over the bridge and between the trees, away from the noisy noises.

Igglepiggle found a quiet part of the garden.

That's better, Igglepiggle.
No noisy noises here.

Then it was time to go home.
Which way, Igglepiggle?

Oh dear.
Igglepiggle didn't know which way to go.
Igglepiggle was lost.

Mi-mi-mi-mi-mi!

Who's here?

Mrs Pontipine looked through her binoculars and saw Igglepiggle lost.

Mi-mi! she said.

Mr Pontipine picked up the trubliphone.

First he called Upsy Daisy.

Then he called Makka Pakka.

Then he called the Tombliboos.

Mi-mi-miiiiiii!

What was Mr Pontipine telling everybody?

Upsy Daaaaaaiiiisy!

Make more
noise singing,
Upsy Daisy!

Clack-clack-clatter-clack!

Make more
noise tidying,
Makka Pakka!

Plink-plonk-bang-bang!

Make more noise playing music, Tombliboos!

Altogether, it was the noisiest noise ever heard in the garden.

What is that noisy noise, Igglepiggle?
Is it your friends?

Follow the noisy noises!

Igglepiggle followed the noisy noises,
between the trees and over the bridge.

Igglepiggle
found his friends.

Igglepiggle loves his noisy friends.
And everybody loves Igglepiggle.

Isn't that a pip?

Once upon a time
in the Night Garden,
Igglepiggle was lost.

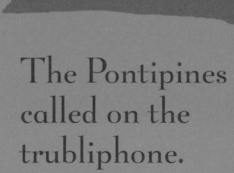

The Pontipines
called on the
trubliphone.

Make more noisy noises everybody!

Igglepiggle followed the noisy noises all the way home.

Igglepiggle loves his noisy friends.

Time to go to sleep everybody.

Go to sleep, Upsy Daisy.

Go to sleep, Makka Pakka.

Go to sleep, Pontipines.

Go to sleep, Tombliboos.

Go to sleep, Haahoos.

Go to sleep Ninky Nonk
and go to sleep, Pinky Ponk.

Wait a minute.
Somebody is not in bed!
Who's not in bed?
Igglepiggle is not in bed!

Don't worry, Igglepiggle...
it's time to go.